LENA SJÖBERG

Bright in the Night

Thames & Hudson

In the night

When night falls, everything is dark.
Or is it?

The moon shines with a pale light. A car
drives along the street, and when its
headlights flash, we see two bright dots
run by. Is it a cat? Or perhaps a fox?
If we stand still for a moment, our eyes
will adjust to the darkness. We can see
twinkling stars in the sky, and sometimes
even the bright belt of stars called the
Milky Way.

The night contains both light and
darkness. Come on a journey to visit
the dark forest, the deep ocean and
the shadows of the city, and discover
everything that glows, glitters and
shines in the night!

The night sky

The twinkling night sky has always been important to humans. The first calendar was invented thousands of years ago, after people studied the changing phases of the moon. Sailors have used the stars to guide them when crossing the ocean, and for people living on land, the moon has been seen as both magical and useful. Under the full moon, tales have been told and harvests have been gathered. Although modern city lights can make it hard to see the stars, the night sky is still fascinating to look at.

Moonlight

The moon doesn't shine by itself. Instead, it reflects the light that is always shining from the sun. Once a month, we can see the whole circle of the moon lit by the sun. This is called a full moon.

Stars

A star may look like a small dot to us, but in fact it's a big ball of burning gas, millions of miles away. In our galaxy, there are hundreds of billions of stars. Like a human, a star is born, grows old and dies, but it lasts for thousands of years. Even the smallest star is much bigger than the Earth, while the biggest one is 2,000 times bigger than the Sun! The Sun is the star that's closest to the Earth.

Moon halo

A halo is a ring of light that can sometimes be seen around the moon. It is caused when light is reflected by ice crystals floating high in the Earth's atmosphere. Similar rings can also appear around streetlights and other bright lights.

LITTLE DIPPER

If you live in the northern hemisphere and want to find the North Star, you can follow a line from the right edge of the Big Dipper to the right edge of the Little Dipper.

THE NORTH STAR

BIG DIPPER

Shooting stars

Shooting stars aren't really stars, but lumps of rock and dust that fly through space. Another name for a shooting star is a meteor. When a meteor touches the Earth's atmosphere, it heats up and glows with a bright trail of light. A good time to see a shooting star is early in August, when the Earth passes through a shower of meteors called the Perseids.

The lights of Jupiter

Using a telescope, astronomers have been able to photograph glowing lights around the north and south pole of the planet Jupiter. On Earth, the same bright glow near the north or south pole is known as the northern lights or southern lights.

Venus

At dusk, we can sometimes see the planet Venus with the naked eye, when it reflects the light of the sun. It seems to shine more brightly than the other stars in the sky, so it is often called the evening star. Venus can also be seen shining at dawn, when it is known as the morning star.

MERCURY

VENUS

EARTH

MARS

JUPITER

SATURN

URANUS

NEPTUNE

SOLAR SYSTEM→

We live here

THE MILKY WAY

The Milky Way

The Milky Way is a galaxy, which is a huge spiral-shaped cloud of stars. One of those stars is our Sun, so the Earth and the other planets in the solar system are all part of the Milky Way too. It is also the home of several hundred billion stars, countless planets, and many enormous clouds of gas, where new stars and planets are born. The Milky Way can sometimes be seen as a hazy white band of light across the night sky.

What's that cloud?

In 1994, there was an earthquake in Los Angeles and all the streetlights went out, leaving the city in darkness. Lots of worried people called the police because they could see a mysterious cloud of stars in the sky. In fact, it was only the Milky Way! The people had never seen it before because the lights of Los Angeles are usually so bright that they blot it out.

Northern and southern lights

Tiny particles from the Sun fly through space and are drawn toward the Earth's magnetic poles. When these particles enter our atmosphere, they combine with the particles there, and create a glowing light called an aurora. It looks like bright ribbons of cloud in many different shades, fluttering across the sky. In the northern hemisphere, the aurora is known as the northern lights. In the southern hemisphere, it's called the southern lights. People travel from all over the world to see these beautiful lights. In some places, such as the far north of Sweden, the lights are visible almost every clear night during the winter.

Signs of things to come

Long ago, the changing shades of the northern lights were used to predict the weather. The northern lights were also sometimes seen as a sign of bad luck to come. The Sámi people of northern Scandinavia believed that it was unlucky to sing or whistle while the northern lights were shining.

This is what the northern lights looked like on a December night in 2015, in a photograph taken in the far north of Sweden. Lots of people thought they looked like a wolf in the sky! In Finnish folktales, the northern lights were said to be caused by a magical fox, whipping up the snow with its tail.

Capturing the northern lights

It's not easy to take a photograph of the northern lights. In pictures, the lights often look green or yellow, but in real life they can be many different shades, including red, blue and purple. The lights also happen in the daytime, but they can only be seen when it's dark.

Glowing eyes

Many animals have eyes that seem to shine in the dark. In fact, they have a special reflecting layer at the back of their eyes. The dim light bounces off this layer and passes through their eyes an extra time, helping them to see at night. The scientific name for this layer is the tapetum lucidum, which means bright blanket. When hit by the light from a car or a flashlight, the eyes of different animals seem to shine in different shades.

Wolf

A wolf's eyes may glow yellow, green or red in the beam from a flashlight or a headlight.

Wild boar

The wild boar is one of the few nocturnal animals that does not have reflectors in its eyes. This means it's hard to see a boar in traffic at night.

Cat

In the darkness, the eyes of brown-eyed cats seem to glow green when the light hits them. The eyes of blue-eyed cats seem to shine red. In the Middle Ages, some people believed that the light from cats' eyes was a reflection of the fires from hell.

Moth

The eyes of some moths reflect the light too.

Lynx

The name "lynx" comes from the Latin word for shine. A long time ago, people used to think that the fur of the lynx could glow in the dark, but that's only a myth.

Owl

Most birds don't have a reflecting layer in their eyes. But owls do, and so do nightjars and some hawks.

Deer

Deer eyes can shine yellow or green in the dark.

Mysterious lights

Have you ever heard of a will-o'-the-wisp? It is a ghostly light that can be seen floating at night, especially over swamps and marshes. Other names for the will-o'-the-wisp include friar's lantern and hinkypunk. In olden times, people invented many strange tales to explain these lights. But what really causes them? Are they some sort of burning gas? An optical illusion? Or a form of lightning? No one knows for certain.

The Lantern Man

Several places in Europe have myths about the Lantern Man. This was a ghostly spirit with a lamp, who haunted marshy places. Sometimes the Lantern Man would lure people to their death in the swamp, but sometimes he would light the way to safety.

Lights around the world

Many parts of the world have legends about mysterious lights.
In Australia, drivers in the Outback are sometimes followed
by the Min Min light. In Japan, strange dancing lights are
blamed on spirits called kitsune. In India, people of the
northern grasslands speak of seeing a moving light called
the chir batti. And in the US, ghostly lights are sometimes
seen close to Route 67 near Marfa, Texas.

Ball lightning

Ball lightning looks like a small floating
ball of white or blue light. People claim to
have seen it near power sockets, chimneys and
railway lines. So far, nobody has found a good
explanation for ball lightning, except that
it often appears during a thunderstorm.

Growing and glowing

In many of the world's forests, a glimmering green glow can be seen among the rocks and roots on the ground. Is it something magical? No, it's a plant called luminous moss. Old names for luminous moss included dragon's gold or goblin gold, because people once believed that it grew where supernatural creatures had buried treasure in the ground.

1 cm

Luminous moss

Luminous moss seems to shine on its own, but it doesn't really. In fact, it's made up of tiny cells that capture the small amount of light from the surrounding area, then reflect it back out again, creating a green shimmer.

Glowing stones

If you shine an ultraviolet light on a diamond, it gives off a blue glow. A similar thing happens with lots of other rocks and gemstones. Amber, for instance, will shine blue, and tugtupite, a rare stone from Greenland, will glow bright red.

Agate

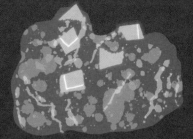

Fluorite

Dolomite

Aragonite

Scapolite

Willemite

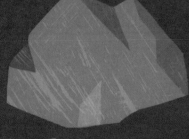

Tugtupite

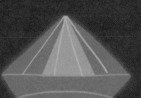

Amber

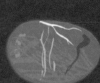

Diamond

Adamite

An ultraviolet lamp can be used to check whether a diamond is real.

Ultraviolet light

Light is made up of waves, which come in different lengths. We see light with different wavelengths as different shades. However, light with a very short wavelength makes shades that we can't see with the naked eye. One of these is called ultraviolet or UV. There are special lamps that give off UV light. If we shine UV light on a piece of amber in a dark room, we won't see the light itself, but we will see the reflected light from the stone, which will look bright blue.

Glowing mushrooms

Over 70 species of luminous mushrooms have
been discovered. Some give off only a faint
glow, but others shine so bright that you could
use them as a reading lamp! The light attracts
insects, which help to spread the mushroom's
spores. It is also believed that mushrooms
glow to scare away animals that might eat
them. When the morning comes, the light
of the mushrooms can't be seen any more.

Honey fungus

Honey fungus grows in many countries. Its roots give off a slight glow and can stretch for miles in every direction. One root system found in the state of Oregon is more than two thousand years old and is one of the largest living things in the world!

Foxfire

Luminous fungus often grows on old trees or fallen branches, making them glow brightly. This kind of light is called foxfire or fairy fire. Hundreds of years ago, foxfire was sometimes brought indoors or carried around like a lamp.

Glowing tracks

Sometimes you can see animal tracks glowing in the dark. This happens because luminous roots are peeping out of the ground where animals have stepped.

Creepy-crawlies

On dark summer nights, you might be lucky enough to see glow worms. In fact, they are not worms but a type of firefly. To attract a mate, the female glow worm sits still and the tip of her tummy glows. In warm countries, different kinds of fireflies are common. When the male firefly wants to find a mate, he flashes his light on and off. There are also luminous centipedes, beetles and snails. Some spiders and butterflies glow under ultraviolet light and chameleons do the same. A rare species of frog, which glows green and yellow under UV light, has also been discovered in Argentina.

Jumping spider

Fire centipede

If a fire centipede is frightened or injured, its body makes glowing slime.

Common glow worm

male

female

Blinking snail

eggs

Butterfly

Railroad worm

The railroad worm is actually the larva of a beetle called Phrixothrix. At night, the glowing dots along its body make it look like a train with lights in the windows.

Common eastern firefly

Polka-dot tree frog

Chameleon

More creepy-crawlies

If you shine ultraviolet light on a scorpion, it glows blue or green. People think that the scorpion's light helps it to find dark places to hide. The giant cockroach also uses light in a clever way. Luminous bacteria live on its body, and in the dark they make the cockroach look just like a poisonous click beetle. With this trick, the bacteria help to scare away animals who want to eat the cockroach.

Termite skyscraper

On the savanna in Brazil, you can see termite mounds looking like glittering skyscrapers in the night. The glow isn't made by termites, but by click beetle larvae, which live in holes on the outside of the termites' mound. Their glowing heads attract smaller insects into the holes, where the larvae can eat them.

Glowing underground

There are several different kinds of luminous worms. Most of them live deep in the ground, and we still know very little about why these worms glow.

Wireworm

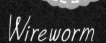

Giant cockroach

TRIES TO LOOK LIKE

Click beetle

Scorpion

Glowing caves

In New Zealand and Australia, there are caves filled with so many glowing insects that the roof looks like it's covered with stars! The insects that live there are known as glow worms, but they are actually a kind of gnat. The larva of this glow worm spins long, glowing threads that hang down from the cave roof like shining beads. Other insects are drawn to the light, and get caught in the sticky threads. Then they become the larva's dinner! When there's the best chance of finding food, the glow worms shine their brightest.

You can visit some of these glowing caves, but you must remember not to disturb the glow worms with loud noises or camera flashes.

gnat

larva

New Zealand glow worm

The New Zealand glow worm hatches from an egg and lives as a glowing larva for up to a year. Then it becomes a pupa, which eventually hatches into a little gnat that lives for only a few days. The pupa gives off a twinkling gleam, while the female gnats glow to attract a male.

Bright birds

Unlike humans, many birds can see ultraviolet light. If we had the same ability, we would be able to see that some birds glow! These birds have parts of their bodies that reflect ultraviolet light. Scientists have discovered that if you shine a UV light on a parrot in the dark, its feathers will appear in new and glowing shades! In many species, the brightest males seem to find a mate more easily.

Atlantic puffin

In UV light, the beak of the Atlantic puffin shines brightly.

beak in UV light

Wilson's bird-of-paradise

The male Wilson's bird-of-paradise is so bright that it seems to glow in the dark, although it doesn't reflect UV light. This bird can only be found on two islands in Indonesia. To attract a female, it flips up its chest feathers to form a bright green collar and does a mating dance.

Blue tit

The blue tit is a bird that lives in parts of Europe and Asia. Although males and females look the same to the naked eye, the patches on the male's head glow in UV light. This is a sign that the male is strong and healthy and will make a good mate for a female.

Barn owl

Some people claim to have seen barn owls glowing like ghosts as they fly through the night. However, nobody has ever been able to prove that luminous owls really exist. Perhaps it's just the bright white feathers of the owl that seem to glow in the moonlight? Another idea is that the owls hunt for food on the ground and get covered in the roots of luminous mushrooms.

Parrots

Parakeet

Deep in the ocean

In the deepest part of the ocean, where the sun cannot reach, it's always night. But look closer, and you can see tiny dots of light glimmering in the darkness. The light comes from fish, squid, shrimp and many other sea creatures that glow. Some of them do it to attract a mate. Others use their light to scare away predators or to find food. Some shine softly and some shoot out glowing clouds. Some even swim high in the water and shine like the moon, so that when predators look up in search of food, they won't be able to see any tell-tale shadows.

Crown jellyfish

When something threatens the crown jellyfish, it flashes like the lights on a police car.

Lanternfish

Vampire squid

Lanterneye fish

The patches underneath the eyes of a lanterneye fish are filled with luminous bacteria. The fish can shine the light in any direction and can make it blink on and off by covering and uncovering it.

Coconut octopus

Clusterwink snail

The clusterwink snail can make its shell flash on and off. The light may be used to make the snail look bigger and to scare away predators.

Lantern shark

Viperfish

Shrimp

Some shrimp can blow out a glowing cloud of slime. This confuses predators and gives the shrimp time to escape.

Angler fish

Ghost shark

Swima worm

Swima worms can throw little balls of luminous slime at predators.

An undersea rainbow

Some luminous sea creatures and plants can make their own light with chemicals inside their bodies. But sometimes their luminous glow can't be seen with human eyes. We have to use UV lights to be able to see the secret rainbow of shades below the sea. Under ultraviolet light, coral, sea pens and sea anemones seem to shine like neon signs! Scientists have discovered that several hundred kinds of fish and shellfish (and one turtle!) can reflect light in this way. One discovery happened when a diver took a photograph of some coral, where a little eel called a false moray was hiding. The eel was hard to see in normal light, but in the diver's UV light, it glowed bright green.

Monocle bream

False moray

Stingray

Seahorse

Brittle star

If the brittle star is attacked, it gives off a powerful light to scare away predators.

Sea anemone

Sea pen

Goatfish

Hawksbill
sea turtle

Chain catshark

Reef stonefish

Red-eye wrasse

Pipefish

Coral

A sparkling sea

In late summer, the ocean near the west coast of
Sweden is filled with tiny little plants called
dinoflagellates or sea sparkles. The sea sparkles
send out flashes of light when they are disturbed.
If you stir the water with your hand or a stick,
it will sparkle with blue or sometimes green
light. This is called the milky seas effect or
mareel. It is also found in the Indian Ocean, and
in the far north of Scotland. Swimming in mareel
is like floating in a sky full of stars!

Comb jelly

The comb jelly is covered in rows of tiny
hairs that glow with light. The comb jelly
eats so much plankton that it can damage
other ocean life. The biggest problem is
caused by the American comb jelly, a species
that has spread very fast all over the world.

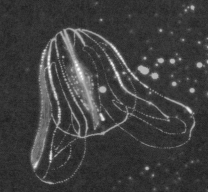

Moon jellyfish

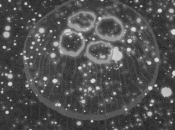

Strange lights at sea

Fishermen and sailors through the ages have talked about magical lights at sea. They have told tales of water sparkling like diamonds, spinning wheels of light and glowing beaches. But there are lots of things that can glow in the dark around a boat, including firefly squid, plankton, sea sapphires and ostracods. There's even the huge and glowing pyrosome, one of the ocean's strangest creatures!

A MILKY GLOW

The milky seas effect is the name for the blue or white glow that happens when masses of tiny glowing plants called sea sparkles gather on the ocean's surface. In 1995, a patch of milky sea off the coast of Africa grew to more than 150 miles long. It was big enough to be seen from space!

AFRICA

PYROSOMES

A pyrosome is a tube-shaped sea creature. It is made up of thousands of tiny animals called zooids. Every zooid pumps water though its body and makes the pyrosome move forward. The pyrosome is one of the brightest glowing creatures in the world. Nobody really knows why the zooids give off light. Maybe it's a way to signal to each other, or perhaps it's to scare off predators. The pyrosome grows longer when the zooids make copies of themselves. The longest pyrosome ever found was 60 feet long, and a dead penguin was once discovered inside a pyrosome that was more than six feet long!

Zooid

Pyrosome

SPARKLING SQUID

For a few months of every year, the sea around Japan turns bright blue with the glow of firefly squid. The squid come to the surface at night time to catch little fish with their glowing tentacles. Different parts of the squid's body can glow, depending on whether it is hunting, hiding from a predator or looking for a mate. In Japan, the firefly squid is thought to make a delicious meal. Lots of people travel to places such as Toyama Bay to see the nets full of sparkling squid being pulled out of the ocean.

SHINING SHRIMP

Ostracods are tiny little shrimp that live on beaches in the Caribbean. At night, they crawl out of the sand to find food, and whenever a wave washes over them, they glow pale blue. The glow is so bright that Japanese soldiers used the light from ostracods to read maps during World War II.

TOYAMA BAY

Firefly squid

Ostracod

GLOWING BEACHES

On some beaches around the world, sea sparkles can make the water glow bright blue. The beach that glows the brightest is on one of the islands of Puerto Rico. Lots of tourists come to see it.

GEMS OF THE OCEAN

Sea sapphires are tiny glowing shrimp that can be found in oceans all over the world. The females are transparent, but the males shine in different shades. They can also turn off their light to make themselves invisible. Scientists think the light helps the males to find a mate. The sea sapphires that swim closest to the surface are yellow, orange or red, while the ones deeper down can be green, blue or purple.

Sea sapphire

Lights on land

We think of night as being dark, but there is lots of light in many places. There are streetlights by the road, a few all-night stores and other buildings, and the lights of cars and trucks passing by. Humans need some light in the darkness to help us move around, but lights at night are not always a good thing. Wild animals can become blinded by the lights of cars on the road. This makes them stand still instead of running away, which can cause accidents.

Fireworks

Fireworks were first invented in China more than a thousand years ago. They were brought to the rest of the world by the explorer Marco Polo in the 15th century.

Night-shining clouds

Sometimes, late in the evening, you can see high clouds that shimmer and shine with a blue light. These are called noctilucent or night-shining clouds. They are made of tiny crystals of ice and dust.

Lighthouses

Many hundreds of years ago, fires were lit on cliff tops to guide ships and warn them about rocks and other dangers. Later, lighthouses were built, with a huge spinning lamp at the top. Lighthouse keepers would live in the lighthouses, making sure the light kept shining. The few lighthouses still working today are automatic and often run on solar power.

Road signs

Road signs are made to reflect light in a similar way to the eyes of cats and other animals. It's important to make sure that the light is reflected straight ahead, so that drivers can see it clearly.

St. Elmo's Fire

During thunderstorms, the electricity in the air can cause bright sparks of light to appear at the top of ships' masts, church towers and other tall pointed objects. This blue or purple glow is called St. Elmo's fire. It has also been spotted at the top of the pyramids in Egypt and on the wings of planes.

Skyglow

Skyglow is the name for the light in the sky that can be seen over cities at night. It is a kind of light pollution.

Las Vegas lights

When seen from space, the brightest city on Earth is Las Vegas, which is full of casinos, hotels and bright neon lights. On top of one of the hotels is the world's most powerful light beam, shining straight at the sky. It's so bright, it can be seen from more than 200 miles away! Las Vegas is also home to the Neon Museum, filled with the city's old signs.

WELCOME TO Fabulous LAS VEGAS NEVADA

City lights

Day and night, all year round, cities shine with light. There is so much light from houses, cars and shops that it can be hard to see the stars in the sky. Too much light can also have other harmful effects. Light pollution can mean that there is hardly any difference between day and night, and this can be disturbing to animals and to humans. Also, wasting light means wasting the planet's resources.

HOTEL

CINEMA

Neon lights

The first neon sign was demonstrated in Paris in 1910.

Satellites

Thousands of satellites are orbiting the Earth, hundreds of miles above our heads. Some of them are used to study space. Others send and receive radio waves, TV or phone signals. When a satellite reflects light from the sun, we can sometimes see it as a shining dot sailing across the sky.

Shop windows

PIZZA

B&B

Save energy!

It's important to do everything we can to help our planet. One small thing that everyone can do is to use low-energy light bulbs. We should also make sure that we turn off lights when we don't need them. That way we can save energy, and it will also be easier to see the things that shine naturally all around us!

Safety reflectors

Cars and bicycles have reflectors so they can be seen at night. You can also buy safety reflectors to wear, to keep you safe when walking in the dark.

The lights of home

Thousands of years ago, people had to make a fire if they wanted light. But lighting a fire was tricky, and the fire had to be watched so that it didn't burn out. When candles, oil lamps and matches came along, life got a little bit easier. And in the early 20th century, when electric lighting became common, it was almost like magic. We're so lucky to be able to light up a room just by flicking a switch!

Moths

Moths often fly around lamps. Some scientists think that this is because insects find their way using the moon as a guide, and the moths think the lamp is the moon. Others believe that moths fly into the lamplight because they think it's light shining through the gaps between leaves.

Taken for granted

We may take light for granted, but in fact we are very lucky. Over a billion people in the world don't have electric lighting.

The future is bright

What will happen in the future? Will scientists invent new ways to create light? And how many glowing animals and plants will we discover for the first time? Whatever happens, we must remember to be kind to our planet and everything that lives there, so that our children and grandchildren will be able to enjoy all the things that glow in the dark.

Glowing ice cream

Someone has already invented ice cream that glows when you touch it with your tongue. It went on sale for the first time in 2013, but it's very, very expensive!

Prize-winning jellyfish

Scientists have discovered why jellyfish glow and are using this to show how our own bodies work. A glowing protein collected from the jellyfish is placed inside the human body and can be tracked from the outside, making it possible to detect diseases. This discovery, which is useful in many different ways, won the Nobel Prize in 2008.

Lighting the way

In the future, it might be possible to make paint or cement that stores energy during the daytime and then glows at night. This could be used for paths in areas without electricity or in stairwells or bathrooms. Perhaps roads in the future will be able to light up when it's icy, to help to keep drivers safe.

Solar streetlights

Some streetlights now use solar power. They store energy from the sun during the day, and use it to shine at night.

Invisible inventions

Do you remember the sea sapphire that can turn invisible? This tiny sea creature is helping scientists to understand how light is reflected. They are using this knowledge to invent new, smart materials. Perhaps one day it could be used to make an invisibility cloak!

Shimmering silk

By mixing the DNA from silkworm caterpillars with DNA from luminous coral and jellyfish, scientists have created silkworms that can spin threads that glow in UV light.

Living streetlights

Perhaps in the future, streetlights will be replaced by glowing trees. Some scientists think they might be able to make a tree glow in the dark by mixing the tree's cells with DNA from luminous moss or fireflies. It might even be possible to grow a plant that glows in a different shade whenever it needs water or if it is sick.

However...

Is it right to experiment with nature like this? Where should we draw the line between ideas that are clever and safe and ideas that are silly or dangerous? Do we really need glowing plants, and what will happen if the luminous plants spread? We need to think carefully about what we want the future to be like.

Good morning!

However dark the night is, it always turns into day. The sky slowly gets brighter. The birds start chirping. The sun rises. If you've been awake in the dark, things that seemed complicated and difficult might suddenly feel a little better. Time to eat breakfast and brush your teeth!

The day is ready to begin! And there are lots of things to do before the evening comes and it's night again.

Bioluminescence

Many insects, fish, shellfish, plankton, bacteria and
mushrooms can create light using chemicals inside their own
bodies. They use this light to find food, scare away predators,
camouflage themselves, or attract a mate. This ability is
called bioluminescence. The word bioluminescence is a mixture
of bios (which means life in Greek) and lumen (which means
light in Latin). Bioluminescence has existed in the ocean for
over 400 million years. It is estimated that over 70 percent
of all sea creatures can glow.

Biofluorescence

Some animals, plants and rocks can absorb ultraviolet light
and turn it into glowing shades of yellow, green, blue, red
and orange. This ability is called biofluorescence. Humans
cannot see this glow with the naked eye, so we need to use an
ultraviolet (UV) light. If we use a UV light in a dark place
(where our eyes are the most sensitive), we can clearly see the
glowing shades being reflected. Scientists think that animals
use biofluorescence to attract prey, scare away predators,
or find a mate.